THIS WALKER BOOK BELONGS TO:

_____

_____

_____

_____

TO AUDREY

FOR ALL THE FUN WE HAD

First published 1995 by Walker Books Ltd
87 Vauxhall Walk, London SE11 5HJ

This edition published 2003

2 4 6 8 10 9 7 5 3

© 1995 Jill Murphy

The right of Jill Murphy to be identified as author/
illustrator of this work has been asserted by her in accordance
with the Copyright, Designs and Patents Act 1988

This book has been typeset in Stone Informal

Printed in China

British Library Cataloguing in Publication Data:
a catalogue record for this book is available from the British Library

ISBN 0-7445-9835-4

www.walkerbooks.co.uk

THE LAST
NOO-NOO

Jill Murphy

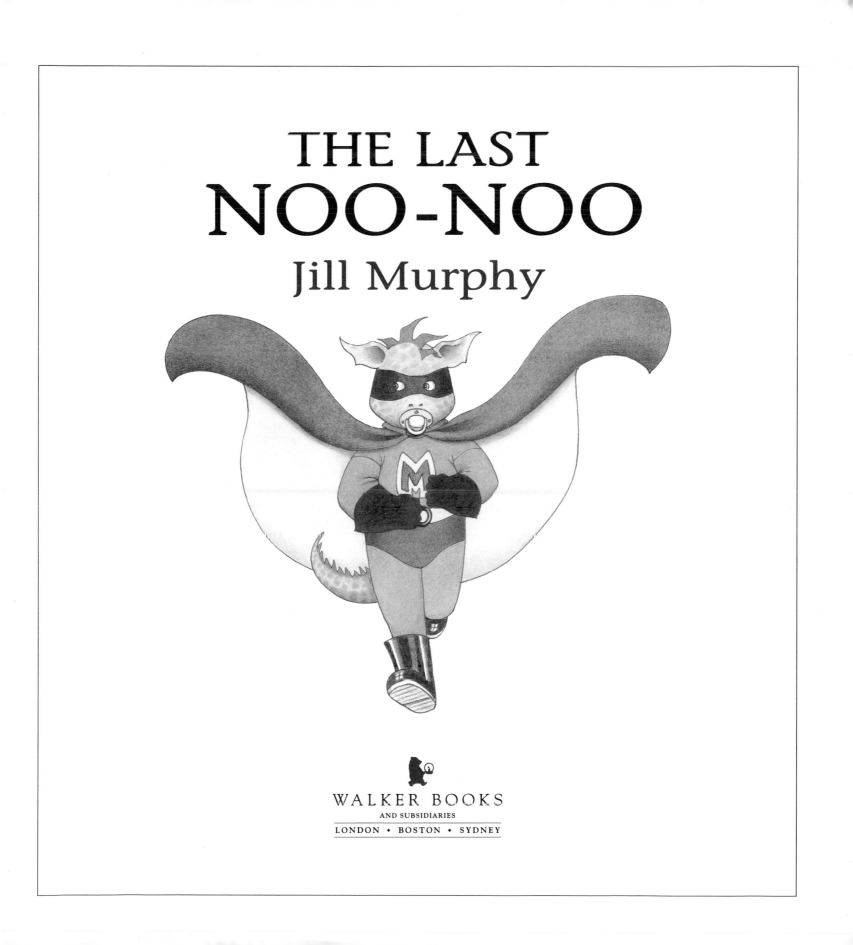

WALKER BOOKS

AND SUBSIDIARIES

LONDON • BOSTON • SYDNEY

Marlon sat on the floor watching TV. Marlon's granny sat in the armchair, watching Marlon. "He's getting too old for that dummy," she said sternly to Marlon's mum.

"It's a noo-noo," said Marlon.

"He calls it a noo-noo," explained Marlon's mum.
"Well, what*ever* he calls it," said Marlon's granny,
"he looks like an idiot with that stupid great *thing*
stuck in his mouth all the time."
"He doesn't have it *all* the time," soothed Marlon's
mum. "Only at night or if he's a bit tired.
He's a bit tired now – aren't you, pet?"
"Mmmmm," said Marlon.

"His teeth will start sticking out," warned Marlon's granny.

"Monsters' teeth stick out anyway," observed Marlon.

"Don't answer back," said Marlon's granny. "You should just throw them *all* away," she continued. "At this rate he'll be starting *school* with a dummy. At this rate he'll be starting *work* with a dummy. You'll just have to be firm with him."

"Well," said Marlon's mum, "I
am *thinking* about it. We'll start
next week, won't we Marlon?
Now you're a big boy, we'll
just get rid of all those
silly noo-noos, won't we?"
"No," said Marlon.
"You see!" said Marlon's
granny. "One word from you
and he does as he likes."
There was no doubt about it.
Marlon was a hopeless case.

Marlon's mum decided to take drastic action.
She gathered up every single noo-noo she could
find and dumped them all in the dustbin
five minutes before the rubbish truck arrived.
But Marlon had made plans just in case the worst
should happen. He had secret noo-noo supplies
all over the house.

There was a
yellow one down
the side of
the armchair,

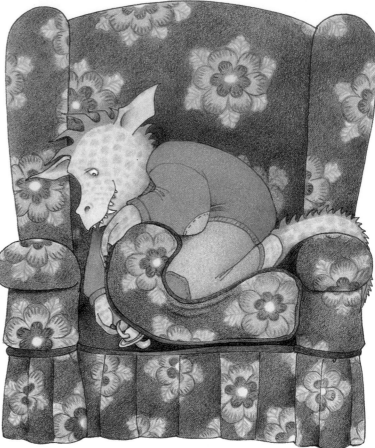

a blue one at the back
of the breadbin,

various different types in
his toy ambulance

and his favourite
pink one was lurking
in the toe of his
wellington boot.

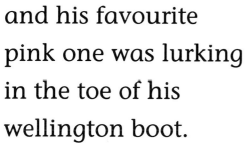

His mother and granny were astonished.
They could not think where he kept finding them.
"You'll be teased when you go out to play,"
warned his granny. "A great big monster
like you with a baby's dummy."
Marlon knew about this already. The other
monsters had been teasing him for ages, but he
loved his noo-noos so much that he didn't care.

The other monsters often lay in wait
and jumped out on Marlon as he
passed by with his noo-noo twirling.
"Who's a big baby, then?"
jeered Basher.
     "Does the little baby

need his dummy, then?" sneered Alligatina.

"Who's his mummy's little darling?"
cooed Boomps-a-daisy.

Marlon always ignored their taunts.

"You're just jealous," he replied.

"You all wish you'd got one too."

Gradually, the secret supply of noo-noos dwindled. Marlon's mum refused to buy any more and they all began to be lost, or thrown away by Marlon's mum. Finally, there was only one left, the pink one. Marlon kept it with him all the time. Either in his mouth or under his pillow or in the toe of his wellington boot, where no one thought to look.

To his delight, Marlon found one extra noo-noo
that his mum had missed. It was a blue one,
which had fallen down the side of his bed and
been covered up by a sock. He knew his best
pink noo-noo wouldn't last for ever, so he
crept out and planted the blue one
in the garden.

All the other monsters decided
to gang up on Marlon. They
collected lots of different bits of
junk and fixed them all together
until they had made just
what they wanted. It was
a noo-noo snatcher.

Then they waited behind a bush
until Marlon came past with his
pink noo-noo twirling.
"Here he comes," said Alligatina.
"Grab it!" yelled Boomps-a-daisy.
"Now!" said Basher.

With one quick hooking
movement, they caught
the ring of the noo-noo
with the noo-noo snatcher
and pulled!

But Marlon clenched his teeth and held on. Monsters have the most powerful jaws in the world. Once they have decided to hang on, that's *it*. Marlon hung on, the monsters hung onto the noo-noo snatcher and there they stayed, both sides pulling with all their monster might.

And there they would *still* be, if Marlon had not decided, just at that very moment, that perhaps he *was* too old to have a noo-noo any more.

So, he let go. And all the other monsters went whizzing off down the road, across the park and into the pond with a mighty splash.

Marlon went home. "I've given up my noo-noo,"
he said. "I sort of threw it into the pond."
"Good gracious me!" exclaimed Marlon's mum,
sitting down suddenly with the shock.
"I told you," said Marlon's granny. "You just
have to be firm."
"Actually," said Marlon, "I've planted one, so I'll
have a noo-noo tree – just in case I change my mind."
"That's nice, dear," said Marlon's mum.

"Nonsense!" said Marlon's granny. "Dummies don't grow on trees. A noo-noo tree! How ridiculous!"

MORE WALKER PAPERBACKS
For You to Enjoy
Also by Jill Murphy

The Large Family books

FIVE MINUTES' PEACE
Winner of the Best Book for Babies Award

All Mrs Large wants is a few minutes' peace in the bath away from the children.
But the little Larges have other ideas!

0-7445-6001-2   £4.99

ALL IN ONE PIECE
Highly Commended for the Kate Greenaway Medal
Shortlisted for the Children's Book Award

While Mr and Mrs Large get ready to go out for the evening, Laura, Lester,
Luke and the baby are busy making a mess!

0-7445-6002-0   £4.99

A PIECE OF CAKE
Mrs Large puts the family on a diet of healthy food and exercise. But when a cake
arrives from Grandma, the family's resolve is sorely tested!

"The illustrations are pure delight… More rueful smiles from mothers everywhere."
The Lady

0-7445-6003-9   £4.99

A QUIET NIGHT IN
Shortlisted for the Kate Greenaway Medal

It's Mr Large's birthday and Mrs Large is planning a quiet night in – without any children.
But in the Large household things rarely go as planned!

"Delectably droll and rumbustious." *The Daily Mail*

0-7445-6000-4   £4.99

Walker Paperbacks are available from most booksellers, or by post from B.B.C.S., P.O. Box 941, Hull, North Humberside HU1 3YQ

24 hour telephone credit card line 01482 224626

To order, send: Title, author, ISBN number and price for each book ordered, your full name and address,
cheque or postal order payable to BBCS for the total amount and allow the following for postage and packing:
UK and BFPO: £1.00 for the first book, and 50p for each additional book to a maximum of £3.50.
Overseas and Eire: £2.00 for the first book, £1.00 for the second and 50p for each additional book.

Prices and availability are subject to change without notice.